FOR YOU

Published in the United States by
Random House Children's Books,
a division of Random House, Inc., New York.

Random House and colophon are registered trademarks
of Random House, Inc.

Visit us on the Web! www.randomhouse.com/kids
www.uglydollbooks.com

Educators and librarians, for a variety of teaching tools,
visit us at www.randomhouse.com/teachers

Library of Congress Cataloging-in-Publication Data
Horvath, David.
Ugly guide to being alive and staying that way /
by David Horvath and Sun-Min Kim.   p.   cm.
ISBN 978-0-375-85702-7 (trade)—ISBN 978-0-375-95702-4 (lib. bdg.)
I. Kim, Sun-Min.   II. Title.
PZ7.H79222Ufg 2009   [E]—dc22   2008005550

MANUFACTURED IN SINGAPORE
10 9 8 7 6 5 4 3 2 1   First Edition

UGLY GUIDE

TO BEING ALIVE
AND STAYING THAT WAY

by David Horvath & Sun-Min Kim

How long is this going to take?

NOT Long.

RANDOM HOUSE NEW YORK

WAGE

ABIMA

ICE-BAT

JEERO

BABO

BABO'S BIRD

BOP 'N' BEEP

MOXY

UGLYWORM

GATO DELUXE

DEER UGLY

TRAY

CINKO

TARGET

WEDGEHEAD

OX

PUGLEE

CHUCKANUCKA

PEACO

BIG TOE

PLUNKO

UGLY GHOST

POE

The Uglyverse may seem busy and confusing, but if you look closer, you'll see that it's actually disorienting and dizzying! But if you open your mind, open your heart, and believe in yourself, you'll find your way just fine.

The best thing about the Uglyverse
is that it can be whatever its inhabitants
want it to be. See the Robot Night School?
It's there because someone thought it up!
If you see something in the real world,
it started as an idea in someone's mind!
So when someone tells you "It's just
your imagination," you're really on to
something!

BiRTH!

& BEING BORN!!!
NO PAIN NO GAIN

Welcome to the Uglyverse!

If you find yourself born into the Uglyverse, it means you're an UGLY! And if that is so, you're going to need this guide to help you through your day-to-day activities. But if you are a bear (if there is such a thing) or other creature, you may want to think twice about doing any of this.

SURPRISE! YOU'RE UGLY

UGLY means unique and special!
UGLY means not afraid to be
who you are on the inside!

The Uglys born at the Ugly Nursery may
all look the same at first, but each one
will become Ugly in their own way soon
enough!

COOKIE
SHAKE
THING

HAND + FOOTPRINTS
WITH "SAFE"
INK

Be prepared! Do you have what it takes?

When you're an Ugly baby, you'll be exposed to all sorts of new and interesting things, such as TV and remote controls. Don't worry about those so much right now. But do begin to worry about your diapers.

SO I ONLY HAVE TO WATCH THIS THING WHILE I'M A BABY, RIGHT? HELLO???

Remote RATTLE

SHOW-2-MAKE U-WANT-TOYS

FONY

You may end up needing a few things to help you get started in the Uglyverse. But remember, life isn't about what you have. It's about what you simply MUST have. That and love. Love mostly, actually.

you'll need some
BABY TOYS

BANK ROBBER PILLOW

NERDY BALL

Expensive ICE-BAT KAIJU MONSTER

STRING THEORY

TOUGH-GUY BALL

IT'S OK!

Square peg in Round Hole self-help Toy

THAT'S LIFE

1-PLAYER BOARD GAME & CHEWY TOY

Peep my kicks

FASHION TREND DOLLY with working Beeper

Rock POP

BABY FOOD MUST-HAVES

TEETN-B-GONE TOOTH FAIRY-SUMMONING CANDY

I.Q. TEST & EAT

MELBA TOAST with HOT PASTRAMI & CHEESE

EAT IT ALL ROBO

AUTO-FEED-ME **ROBO** FRUIT CUP

NO-NONSENSE FRUIT JAR

very close 2 Being **MILK**

SECRET FORMULA

HELP WASH IT DOWN!

BURGER PREP JUICE

HELPS BABY DEAL WITH it.

BURGER PREPARATION JUICE

In the Uglyverse, kids spend most of their time getting ready for the days ahead. . . . Lots of sitting behind desks and learning all about things to better prepare you for the days ahead of those days ahead. And those days will be spent preparing for the end of your days. Basically, be prepared! Don't forget to learn how to go potty along the way.

I took a wrong turn.

LITTLE POTTY TIME

Little POTTY

UGLY STROLLERS

You'll need a ride, too!

Choose wisely.

COIN-OP WEDGEHEAD
PRICEY WICEY

SOUNDPROOF
HANDSFREE LX

TOTAL
CONTROL
DELUXE

NOTHING ON
TUNE OUT
2000

EMPLOYEE-ONLY DOOR
SMASHER

EATY FEED SPEEDER

When you get a little
bit older, you'll be able to walk, talk, and climb
onto those really hard metal rides they have at
the playground. Watch your teeth when you slip
on those. The best thing about
being a kid is playtime!

3

Different types of kids

WAITING for the right moment to PICK

ALSO WAITING

WAITING TO SEE PHOTOS

KIDS' GAMES

RUN!

ATM HIDE + SEEK

I DARE ME.

ONE-PLAYER TRUTH OR DARE

YUP, It's the future again.

THIS SIDE THAT SIDE

TIME TRAVEL

Hey!

BUG COLLECTING

IS IT REALLY LIKE THIS?

I HAVE A JOB MAKE-BELIEVE (AKA: NAPTIME)

NOBODY'S Looking FOR me!

HIDE-AND-SEEK AND SNACK

GRADE? OH, LIKE F—?

Grade school in the Uglyverse is the most important part of an Ugly's education. They teach you everything under the sun! Then all you have to do is remember all of it and take really hard tests. Once that's over, you take naps! It's a dreamy world where sleep meets smarts.

TEACHER CHART

NEW! NOW WITH SECRET CODE!

REAL!

MAKES YOU SMARTER

EYES IN BACK OF HEAD

WAS LEANING ON CHALKBOARD

CHALK FAIRY DUST

BIG MONEY STASH! TEACHERS ARE RICH!!!

Teachers are the best-paid professionals in the Uglyverse! That's why they dress so snazzy!

When you get hungry at school, you've got two choices.

① BRING IT FROM HOME

② GO HOME WITH A TUMMY PAIN

Grade school is filled with very young little Uglys, so the teachers will probably skip the stuff about alternate universes and string theory. And Silly String theory.

BULLIES

AND OTHER REASONS TO

RUN

You really have to watch out for bullies. Why? They are very sensitive and need your love and care. Bullies are bullies because they are afraid. Unfortunately, they are not afraid of you. So run.

TYPES OF BULLIES

The best way to avoid bullies is a really great pair of running shoes. Or get the . . .

BULLY-B-GONE KIT

☐ ALSO INCLUDES BANDAGES

Junior high in the Uglyverse is kinda scary at first. Grade school was lots of fun and lots of naps. But in junior high, they don't give you anywhere soft to take your naps. So you end up drooling on the desk a lot. The good news is, the material you will be learning is super exciting!

The young Uglys in junior high start to show off
their individuality through fashion and hairstyles.

By the time Uglys reach
the end of junior high,
they've figured out if they want to be a
sci-fi nerd or a role-playing gamer, or
maybe get one of those astronaut jobs.

THE UGLY HIGH SCHOOL FACTS

I got AN F-.

The Ugly High School is where things really start to get interesting! There's so much to learn, and Uglys start to get a real feeling for what they want to do with their life.

But I don't WANT good grades!

Those can Lead to a good JOB!

To help the Uglys make the most of their time, the Ugly High School has hired highly trained professionals with the knowledge and wisdom necessary to mold young minds.

I want to make Birdhouses!

The Truant Force helps you remain in your seat so you're free to focus on what you're really interested in. Just look at all the exciting classes!

There's no such thing as being cool in the Uglyverse.
Everyone is a nerd. "Nerd" means being excited about
something and not being afraid to show it! These guys
show it the most.

Role-Playing Gamers

① wears costume in his mind.
② HAS 300 HP to spare.
③ CAN PAINT SMALL LEAD FIGURES IN TOTAL DARKNESS.

COSPLAYERS!!!

① sings ANIME ending songs for you.
② BELIEVES IN THE LEGENDARY WARD OF SHIBUYA. IT'S REAL!
③ LOOKS JUST LIKE THINGS YOU ARE TOTALLY UNAWARE OF.

UGLY COLLEGE

AT

PRICE HIKE UNIVERSITY

cheat notes R BAD

(OR P.U.)

P.U.!!! That stands for "Price Hike University." Price Hike, the Uglyverse's leading retail chain, has opened its very own college!

Within these great walls, Uglys learn what they need to make it in the real world. They even learn how to make it in the fake world.

P.U.

YOU

SHOULD KNOW BETTER

ENROLL TODAY!

Burger worm

OVER DUE TEXT BOOK FISH

BOOK FISH CAN READ

THIS is a college?

I know, right? So impressive.

OX & WEDGEHEADS

SNACK ATTACK VAN

CALL'N PAY A LOT

SNACK ATTACK VAN

Join secret societies
at your own risk!

At our own risk too!

College is where you learn what you need to
know to succeed at your dream job. If you
notice some strange Uglys wandering around
outside the campus, those are the ones who
will open their own business. So study hard
and you'll be able to work for them! To
make this bearable, there's the Ugly Glee
Club. Enjoy!

WHAT TO DO AFTER COLLEGE

Here comes that awkward moment... I need to ask what there is to eat around here.

STAY HOME?

Once you graduate from college in the Uglyverse, there's going to be a special time when you realize you don't want to do the thing you were studying to do. This is called move-back-home time.

I'M BAAAAACK!

This is the happiest part of life for parents. It's like having kids all over again! And just like the first time around, the kids don't pick up their own socks!

NOW what.

I think I know.

LOAN DUE NOW

If you're an Ugly living at home, you may want to get a fake job. Creativity counts!

WHAT DO YOU WANT
TO DO WITH YOUR LIFE?
The choices are UNLIMITED!
A few are good ones!

OK

REAL

FACT-CHECKER

SAILOR

IT'S A DESK JOB, RIGHT?

1st MATE

You can be anything you want in life! All you have to do is believe in your dream and know in your heart it is possible.

It's that easy.
Kind of.

YOU CAN DO IT!

WEIGHT-LIFTER VIDEO STAR

YEAH, you need some work.

FASHION CONSULTANT

As you can see, there's no limit to how one might want to spend one's days, day in . . . day out. Over and over. But to really succeed, you're going to need these four things. . . .

THINGS YOU NEED TO SUCCEED

☐ OFFICEY-LOOKING PLANT

☐ TONS OF THOSE FAKE BOOKS Behind you

☐ The green "I'M SO RICH!" LAMP

☐ CLICKITY-CLACKY TOY THING

TOYS

Once college is over and done with, Uglys usually begin to collect toys. The trick is to buy three of everything. One to open, one to keep in the box, and one for when others want to play. (Stunt double.)

The tricky thing about toys is that it's really hard to find the ones you want. They only make a few million, so hurry!

8-BIT VIDEO GAMES

Video games are a great way to play all day! The most popular game in the Uglyverse is Help Others 2000!

HELP OTHERS?

WE'RE NOT PLAYIN'!!!

HIGH SCORE!!!

DELIVER ICE CREAM! HELP OLD FOLKS!
U NEED HELP!

90% OFF CLOSE-OUT

CLEVER MONEY-SPENDER TOY

FIGHT with FRIENDS 17

ACTUALLY HURTS your feelings!
NOT TO BE USED
U REALLY WANNA CRY?!!

There was once a video game where you battled your friends, but it didn't sell very well.

HELPS YOU GROW ACCUSTOMED TO THE IDEA OF FIGHTING!

BATTLE TOYS FOR BOYS

IF COWS FIGHT, SO SHOULD YOU!

Just remember, if you want to play, you have to wait all day!

Do any games MAKE YOU LESS VIOLENT? GARDENER 2000?

your game is now mine.

PLEASE DON'T trample me!!!

GAME SYSTEM HERE IN 3 WEEKS. YOU CAN'T HAVE IT!!!

RUN!!! when doors open

OPEN AT MIDNITE OIL

LOVE

Love is in the air.

THE MOST AWESOME POWER IN THE uglyverse.

Love is the most powerful force in all the Uglyverse! Some love their pets, some love their hobbies, and some love the Ugly sitting next to them. Just watch out for Wedgehead and Ox's Tunnel of Love ride. It's kind of pricey and the boats leak.

TUNNEL OF LOVE

GOOD LUCK

ESCAPE EXIT

ARE we sinking?

WAIT, this isn't the tunnel of Mega-Riches!

NEXT

What do you love? In the Uglyverse,
whatever you hold in your mind will
come to you!

You don't need a psychic to find love!
Unless you are in love with one.

YOU'LL BE WANTING A
CAREER!
APPLY YOURSELF

Time to go job-hunting!

The key to a successful resume review is a straight face and no bad smells.

OFFICE SUPPLIES

- [ ] PENCIL SHARPENER
- [ ] "TAKE ALL OF THOSE PAPER CLIPS AND NOTEPADS HOME" BAG
- [ ] MISTAKE SHREDDER
- [ ] STATE-OF-THE-ART COMPUTER
- [ ] ONE OF THOSE TALKING 1,000-COLOR PENS
- [ ] BOSS-PROXIMITY CHECKER 2000
- [ ] "I'M AT THE MEETING" DUMMY
- [ ] LOOK-BUSY MEETING KIT WITH GOALPOST
- [ ] OFFICE CHAIR WITH ESCAPE HATCH

If you're going to work in an office,
you're going to need a few things.
Like breaks!

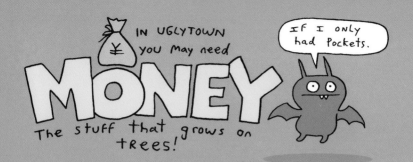

After you work for a few weeks, someone
will hand you a piece of paper. That's money!
You get more when you work some more.

Just remember to save your money.
That way it won't be gone.

If you want to do well in the Uglyverse, you should learn as much as you can about how to save money, and how to make the money you already have GROW!

Or you can try the ALL-A-Loan bank guy.

Just be careful not to use it all on games and toys.

NOW THAT YOU HAVE A LIFE, LET'S GO
SHOPPING
AND SPEND AWAY YOUR HARD-EARNED $!

> I CAN get this for TWICE the price at Price Hike!

> Oooh, Fancy. Hey, WAIT.

SUPER UGLY VCR game Hi-TECH HI-FI! INCLUDES TAPES!

If you want to go shopping in the Uglyverse, you'll definitely want to check out PRICE HIKE! They have everything anyone could ever need, from super hi-tech VCR games to mixmaster turntables!
And if you need to return something, the wait is only a few hours long!

> There's A re-restocking Fee.

> Come ON! It has WOOD PANELING on the SIDE!

> Did I Leave the RADIO ON?

You're NEXT

RETURNS YEAH, RIGHT

Turntable DX

PARKING 101

One important piece of advice about parking in the Uglyverse: don't let anyone know you want to park in their spot! If they see you looking for a space, they'll stay in their car all day! Just act natural.

Drive casual.

Once you make it to Price Hike, you'll want to walk over to the aisle of your choice and pick out the item you're looking for. Not so fast! Odds are, the item you want is somewhat popular. If that's true, you're going to have to get it from the back room. Only, you aren't allowed back there. But no worries.

BACK ROOM CHECKLIST

☐ ORANGE Price Hike SHIRT (TRY one on in the FASHION-PASSION AISLE.)

Hello, my fake name is _____.

☐ NAME TAG (OFFICE SUPPLIES)

what A mess. ☑

☐ CLIPBOARD

OH NO, I'm getting sleepy.

what.

☐ YOUR very BEST "I BELONG HERE" FACE

☐ Lookout PAL

☐ your BEST RUNNING shoes (IN CASE YOU get BUSTED)

Price Hike

☐ STORE HAT (you can get a Paper one at the FooD court.)

If you dress the part and keep a straight face, you'll be paying for the exact item you came in for in no time!

A CLIPBOARD SAYS I CAN FIRE YOU!

ok ☑

keep the running shoes on. Those cops from Ugly Guide #1 will be here very soon.

LUXURY ITEMS

Price Hike doesn't have everything, though. For luxury items, you need to find the fancy schmancy shops!

GAZILLION DOLLARS

Five Bucks

{REAL}

{FAKE}

Watch out for fakes! They are made by the same folks who make the real ones! What a bargain!

I'm the cool DOOR MAN. You want to shop here?

I just want one of your shopping BAGS to carry around.

me too! HA HA!

If you do buy
luxury items . . .

. . . please make sure you're
using the money you've saved for a
rainy day . . . and not the money
you've saved for the rest of your days.

You are what you eat!
So Jeero must be a bag of flavor snaps
and a loaf of A LOT OF DOUGH bread.
But if you really think about it, eating
lots of veggies instead of sweets means
you get to eat far more birthday cakes.

JUNK FOOD

ADD MILK IF U DARE
BABO-OS
NOT FRUIT!

UGLY DRINKY
Make you want to run AWAY!!
DUDE, WE WET, BRO!

UGLY SPORT
is sitting a sport?

UGLY DINNER TV
FLAVOR #51 COOKIE with STEAK & PEAS on the side
Yeah!
Hey, so if you really EAT this, Don't go for seconds, OK? Really.
MEAL-OH-MY!!!!

Junky or healthy? It's up to you!

HEALTH FOOD

WAGE'S OAT BARN
I'M MADE IN A BARN
You go first.

UGLY THINKY-DRINKY
100% JUICE, MOSTLY
OH, I get it.

UGLY WATER
NO FLUORIDE! Some WATER!
ALL WET

UGLY MEAL AT HOME
INCLUDES entire FAMILY, TABLE, CHAIRS, AND 2 EXTRA hours.
WAIT, WHAT?
ANY FOOD?
HEY, YOU good for you?

The Uglyverse is full of a
gazillion types of food.
Some are good for you!
Others taste great!
Just watch out for
Pay Phone Burger.
So good! So bad.

PAY PHONE BURGER

IT'S 4 U!

Press 3 for me.

Phone Bill

IT'S FOR YOU

I'M FINE.

A little sleepy.

THIN

FAT

LiFE'S UGLY MYSTERIES EXPLAINED!

The great unknown!

NO CLUE PAD

2+2=

mysteries start with really old books.

what dat.

There's more to the Uglyverse than what they teach you in school. Unless you've been to mystery school!

I'M A QUANTUM MECHANIC.

The Uglyverse is made up of several multiverses.

And all of those universes exist in the same space!

I MAKE MY OWN HAIR STAND UP.

UGLY GHOST

In an alternate Uglyverse,
Babo is still Babo, but he's purple!

In the Uglyverse, nothing really exists
until it is observed.

Which means you had
better go observe
your homework!!!

YOUR VERY OWN HOUSE

GHOSTS AND ALL!!!

House has ghosts? ye Bought it? HA!

NEXT

one of those old haunty paper MAP things

I'M TOO OLD for this stuff!

Experience? I just graduated!

Hire me ↑

RESUME ☑

Time to buy a home of your very own! The Uglyverse has some of the best real estate agents around! See them lined up, ready to sell you one of these fantastic deals?

Boo hoo

What's with the ghost?

Ok, so there's a little detail we may have left out.

Every house in the Uglyverse is haunted! But not to worry. You'll probably get along just fine with your special guest.

Actually, you'll be the guest if he should ask. Just play nice. It will be OK. Really. Best of luck. Bye.

JUST MARRIED

If you're going to attend a wedding in the Uglyverse, you're going to want to remember a few things. Always dress up really nice, always be polite, and always avoid the snack bar fish cakes. Oh, and watch out for those cans on the back of the wedding mobile.

WEDDING MUST-HAVES

- ☐ SOMETHING ELSE to EAT
- ☐ LOUD CELL PHONE
- ☐ GIFT *50% OFF PIZZA-LAND*
- ☐ SO-SO FOOD
- ☐ SO-SO SIDE DISHES
- ☐ EXTRA TUX IN CASE you spill
- ☐ EXTRA WATER BALLOONS
- ☐ Let them speak NOW—OBJECTION HAND PUPPET
- ☐ Something to read *ALL THINGS A~Z*
- ☐ WHODUNIT KIT
- ☐ VIDEO CAMERA *BETA*
- ☐ ICE-BAT ICE SCULPTURE

All you have to do is stay awake!
The rest is easy.
Don't bring a
watch.

I think I LEFT the VCR ON!

Here for the FOOD.

SAME here.

MUST tinkle

KiDS!
The Little Uglys

They grow so fast!
It's true, in the Uglyverse, Little Uglys grow almost overnight!

They grow so fast.

EAT IT ALL AND SO WILL YOU!

you too, PAL.

Being a Little Ugly is pretty easy living. Eat all day. Sleep all night. Take long naps. Or was it cry all night and never sleep?

Let's see... Cry all night, then go to sleep almost never. Ready, go.

Dress them up nice and warm! They'll last longer!

BABYSITTER 2000

The Uglyverse is filled with many wacky
inventions. The Babysitter 2000
is an all-new state-of-the-art
Little Ugly sitter. Or you could go the
old-fashioned route.

WANT to
PLAy
cookie house?

Yeeeeeeah,
TOMORROW!

BABYSITTER 2000 DELUXE

Make sure everyone buckles up!
Especially if you are riding around in
a carnival game-themed minivan.

To pass the time as you pass
the security checkpoint, try
playing some road trip games!
That will keep everyone's mind off
of the flying debris!

STRESS, FEAR,

AND AWESOME GADGETS

what if I worry about something!?

what if they stop making CD players? I have over 9 CDs.!!!

Worry and stress are an Ugly's worst enemy! When they worry, they aren't able to focus on making their dreams come true.

The good news is, there's nothing to fear!

I FEAR TINY WORMS.

Please Don't see me. Please Don't see me.

Computers can cause a little worry,
but they are pretty awesome, so it's Ok.

Some Uglys are scared of ghosts, and
Ugly Ghosts are worried that there's
no such thing!

BUT WHAT IF YOU'RE AN UGLY DRAGON?

(I KNOW, BUT WHAT IF?)

I have a life TOO, ya know.

Ugly Dragons are a very special type of creature found in the Uglyverse.

Actually, I'm not SO into flying.

I'm more INTO TOY CARS.

vroom

They like to hide up in the caves of Ugly Dragon Mountain.

UGLY DRAGON MOUNTAIN

Poe, a very young Ugly Dragon, lives by himself at Poe's Cave Cove.

Poe's Cave Cove is just north of your present location.

That's where he keeps his massive collection of toys and little race cars.

Ugly Dragons love the drive-thru, so keep a lookout for them! If you find a fry in your hair, that's them.

When things start to slow down
a little, others may call you "old,"
but age is in the mind!

In the Uglyverse, how old you
are and how old you feel are up to you!

Still, if you feel like taking it easy, there's always retirement! They have some pretty neato games to play when you retire.

SEE YOU NEXT TIME

If you were lucky enough to be born into the Uglyverse, then you know the party is never over!

WAIT, I WASN'T DONE WITH THAT!

Plus the cookies are so good, you'll want to keep coming back for more.